you are my merry

Written and illustrated by
Marianne Richmond

sourcebooks
jabberwocky

Published by Sourcebooks Jabberwocky, an imprint of Sourcebooks, Inc.
P.O. Box 4410, Naperville, Illinois 60567-4410
(630) 961-3900
Fax: (630) 961-2168
www.sourcebooks.com

Library of Congress Cataloging-in-Publication data is on file with the publisher.

Source of Production: Leo Paper, Heshan City, China
Date of Production: July 2015
Run Number: 5003958

Printed and bound in China.
LEO 10 9 8 7 6 5 4 3 2 1

To my family,
my love and my joy.

Welcome
Merry Christmas,
our favorite time of year,

full of joy and laughter,
friendship and good cheer.

It's the season of *wonder*

and **FUN** make-believe.

And for *dreaming* of ways

we will GIVE and RECEIVE.

But I already know
what you are to me.

My BEST
gift of all
is not under
the tree.

You are *my* **silly**
when we play
in the snow,

making angels with wings

and snowballs to throw.

You are *my* sweet
when we make
YUMMY treats,

like cookies with sprinkles
and gingerbread eats.

You are my **cozy** when we snuggle at night,

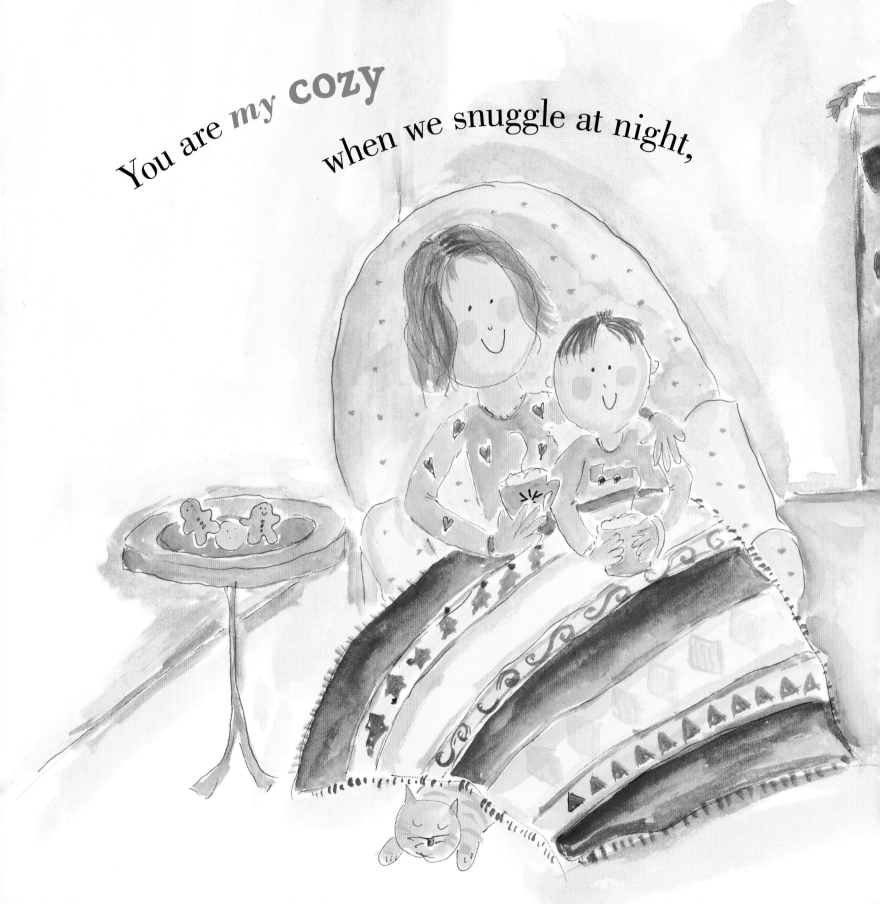

with marshmallow cocoa
by warm firelight.

And you are *my* **jolly**
when we visit the mall,
to tell Santa the toy
you'd like **MOST** of all.

North Pole

"Will you tell him," you ask,

"I've been helpful
to you, though
some days I know
I do what I do?"

Yes, you are *my* **joy,**
all year throughout,
my **kiss** and *my* **cuddle**
without any doubt.

You are *my* **thankful**
when we make time to SHARE
GOODNESS with others
to show how we CARE.

And you are
my sparkle
when together we go
see neighborhood lights
or your holiday show.

You're *my* **glee** and
my **giggle**

with friends far and near,
making memories to fill us
with laughter all year.

You're *my* **love** and *my* **joy**—
a gift I'll always carry

through Christmas
and FOREVER

you *are my* merry

ABOUT THE AUTHOR

Beloved author and illustrator Marianne Richmond has touched the lives of millions for nearly two decades through her award-winning books and gift products that offer meaningful ways to connect with the people and moments that matter.